Taffy Trouble

Candy Fairies

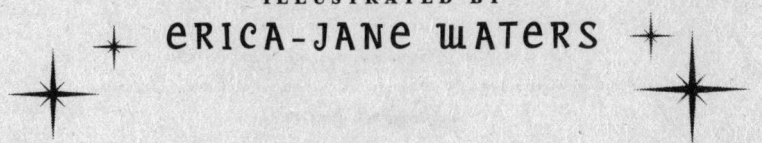

Taffy Trouble

HELEN PERELMAN

ILLUSTRATED BY
ERICA-JANE WATERS

ALADDIN
NEW YORK LONDON TORONTO SYDNEY NEW DELHI

This book is a work of fiction. Any references to historical events, real people, or real places are used fictitiously. Other names, characters, places, and events are products of the author's imagination, and any resemblance to actual events or places or persons, living or dead, is entirely coincidental.

ALADDIN

An imprint of Simon & Schuster Children's Publishing Division

1230 Avenue of the Americas, New York, NY 10020

First Aladdin paperback edition June 2015

Text copyright © 2015 by Helen Perelman

Illustrations copyright © 2015 by Erica-Jane Waters

Also available in an Aladdin hardcover edition.

All rights reserved, including the right of reproduction in whole or in part in any form.

ALADDIN is a trademark of Simon & Schuster, Inc., and related logo is a registered trademark of Simon & Schuster, Inc.

For information about special discounts for bulk purchases, please contact Simon & Schuster Special Sales at 1-866-506-1949 or business@simonandschuster.com.

The Simon & Schuster Speakers Bureau can bring authors to your live event. For more information or to book an event contact the Simon & Schuster Speakers Bureau at 1-866-248-3049 or visit our website at www.simonspeakers.com.

Book design by Karina Granda

The text of this book was set in Baskerville Book.

Manufactured in the United States of America 0515 OFF

2 4 6 8 10 9 7 5 3 1

Library of Congress Control Number 2015935785

ISBN 978-1-4814-0614-7(hc)

ISBN 978-1-4814-0613-0 (pbk)

ISBN 978-1-4814-0615-4 (eBook)

For Sigal and Lisa Goldstein,
the sweetest friends and fans

Contents

CHAPTER

1

Nillie's Call

Cocoa the Chocolate Fairy was in a hurry. She had just read a sugar fly message from Candy Castle. The note was from Princess Lolli, the ruling fairy princess of Candy Kingdom. Cocoa didn't waste a second and flew straight to the castle. She hoped everything was all right. It wasn't every day that

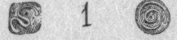

she got a sugar fly message from Princess Lolli!

When Cocoa arrived at Candy Castle, she was very nervous. Her Caramel Fairy friend Melli was usually the one to worry. But this time Cocoa's stomach was fluttering as fast as her wings!

The castle guard told Cocoa to go to the throne room. There, Cocoa was happy to see three of her good friends: Raina the Gummy Fairy, Melli the Caramel Fairy, and Dash the Mint Fairy.

"Princess Lolli will be with you in one moment," the guard told them. Cocoa looked at her friends. They all shared the same worried expression.

"Is Berry all right?" Cocoa asked. She saw

that her Fruit Fairy friend was not in the throne room.

"She's on her way," Dash said. "She's late as usual."

Just then Berry flew into the room. She was panting. "I got here as fast as I could," she said. "Did I miss anything?"

Cocoa could tell that Berry was worried something was wrong. Berry was late to everything because she always had to look her best. She usually arrived in a stylish outfit, with matching sparkling fruit chews in her hair. Cocoa saw that Berry had not bothered to change out of her gardening clothes. She had come straight from her work in Fruit Chew Meadow.

"We're waiting for Princess Lolli," Raina

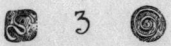 3

said to Berry. "We were told she would be here any minute."

Melli bit her lip. "This doesn't feel right. Something is wrong."

Cocoa agreed. Something about this meeting made her feel uneasy.

"Hello, my sweets," Princess Lolli said as she entered the room. "Thank you all for coming so quickly." Her expression changed as she sat down on her throne. "I have gotten sad news from Nillie," she said.

Cocoa gasped. Nillie was the gentle sea horse who watched over the Vanilla Sea. Cocoa and her friends had met the sea horse when they were traveling across the Vanilla Sea to solve the gooey goblin mystery. At first the Candy Fairies had been scared of her. They had all

heard stories about the sea monsters in the Vanilla Sea and thought Nillie was one of them. It turned out that Nillie was a kind and beautiful sea horse. Cocoa and her friends had learned that Nillie herself had made up those sea monster stories to keep the waters safe for the animals and creatures living there.

"Is Nillie hurt?" Raina asked.

"No," Princess Lolli said. "Thank goodness, she is fine. But she is very concerned about what is going on in the North Sea."

"Oh, hot caramel," Melli said.

"Nillie needs our help," Princess Lolli went on. "She has asked me to send the five Candy Fairies she met in the Vanilla Sea."

"She asked for *us*?" Cocoa asked. She could hardly believe her ears.

Princess Lolli nodded. "You all made a very good impression on her."

"What can we do for her?" Dash asked. She flew closer to Princess Lolli.

Princess Lolli put her arm around Dash. "Nillie says that the caramel turtles have reported trouble in the North Sea. It seems there is a troll named Gargo hunting the Sea Fairies' candy. He is taking the chocolate clams and salted caramel coral."

"Sour sugars!" Raina exclaimed.

"That can't be good," Berry added.

Princess Lolli lowered her head. "No, it is not good. When the troll steals the chocolate clams and the salted caramel coral, he ruins the balance of the salt in the water. Not only is it bad for the troll to be stealing the candy, but he is also making the water unsafe for the Sea Fairies."

"Not to mention what will happen to the saltwater taffy," Dash added.

"Dash!" Cocoa scolded.

Princess Lolli patted Dash on the back. "Dash is right. This is a big concern. If the troll keeps this up, there also won't be the right amount of salt in the water to make the taffy."

"Why did Nillie think of us?" Cocoa asked.

Princess Lolli stood up. "Because you were the ones who solved the gooey goblin mystery," she said. "And because she knows you know the secret to tricking a troll."

Cocoa stood a little taller. She knew Princess Lolli was talking to her. After all, she was the one who had been brave enough to go to Black

Licorice Swamp with Princess Lolli when Mogu the troll was stealing her chocolate eggs.

"I know you fairies can help Nillie," Princess Lolli said. "This job will require a different kind of magic." She paused. "You will have to go underwater to help the Sea Fairies."

"Like mermaids?" Dash blurted out.

"Sea Fairies are not mermaids," Raina told Dash. She gave her a stern look.

No one knew the Fairy Code Book better than Raina, and Cocoa was certain that her friend was about to tell them a fact about Sea Fairies.

"Sea Fairies aren't mermaids, because they don't have tails," Raina went on. "They have special water wings."

"Yes, that's right, Raina," Princess Lolli said. "Nillie's sea-salt magic will turn your wings to water wings. But you have to be very careful when using the sea-salt magic. Your wings will only be water wings while the sea-salt magic lasts." She looked each fairy straight in the eye. "You must promise me that you will each listen and obey Nillie's words. Sea-salt magic is very powerful."

"Sure as sugar, you can count on us." Cocoa spoke for all her friends. She knew that they had to get to the North Sea and stop Gargo!

2

Salt-Crystal Orb

There is more I need to tell you," Princess Lolli said. She waved to the fairies to come closer.

Cocoa flew up to Princess Lolli's throne. All the fairies stood in a tight circle. Cocoa could feel how nervous they all were. As she watched Princess Lolli she had the feeling this trip was more important than they realized.

"We can handle trolls," Cocoa told Princess Lolli. "We aren't afraid."

"Maybe some of us are," Melli muttered.

Cocoa nudged Melli. "Nillie has asked us for help. She helped us when we needed it in the Vanilla Sea. We will be there for her, too."

"I suppose," Melli said. "I will try to be brave."

We all need to be brave, Cocoa thought. She wasn't sure how the sea-salt magic would work or how it would feel to be underwater. She fluttered her wings. She always had to be so careful *not* to get her wings wet. When a Candy Fairy's wings were wet, the water weighed the wings down and it was difficult for the fairy to fly. Being underwater would be a very strange feeling.

Princess Lolli squeezed Melli's hand. "I am counting on all of you," she said. "This is not an easy task."

"But we can do it!" Berry burst out.

"Sure as sugar!" Dash added.

Cocoa was so proud of her friends. She knew they were all going to be helpful and brave.

"I have something for you," Princess Lolli said. She flew over to a chest in the corner of the room and lifted out a small sugar box. Then she reached into the box and pulled out a necklace. "Raina, do you know what this is?"

Cocoa eyed the orb hanging from the licorice-braided necklace. The beautiful white crystal was glowing and sparkling. She had never seen anything quite like it.

"*So mint!*" Dash exclaimed.

"Sweeter than chocolate," Cocoa mumbled.

"That is the most scrumptious jewel I have ever seen," Berry said.

Raina moved closest to Princess Lolli. "Is that a salt-crystal orb from Ice Cream Isles?" she asked. "Those are very rare and very special." She moved one step closer. "I've only read about them. I've never seen one."

"It is *sugar-tastic*," Melli cooed. "Is that Prince Scoop's?"

Prince Scoop was Princess Lolli's husband. He was from Ice Cream Isles and had recently married Princess Lolli. All the Candy Fairies liked him very much.

"Yes, this is Scoop's," Princess Lolli replied. "He wanted me to give this to you. This jewel has special powers and will help keep all of you safe."

"I've read that salt crystals have helped many fairies in some sour situations," Raina said.

Princess Lolli nodded. "This jewel can save lives, so please don't lose it! One of you must be wearing it at all times during your journey." She handed the necklace to Cocoa. "Do you want to wear it?"

Cocoa blushed and took the necklace.

"When you wear this crystal, I will be able to watch you," Princess Lolli explained. "Just in case of an emergency."

Melli's eyes widened. "An emergency? Sweet sugars, I hope we don't have any emergencies!"

Cocoa smiled and gave Melli a hug. She slipped the necklace on. It began to glow.

"Please take good care of this necklace . . . and of one another," Princess Lolli said.

Cocoa held the crystal in her hand. It was smooth and glowed with a soft white light. "Thank you," she whispered. "We will take special care of this . . . and of one another."

"How do we reach Nillie?" Raina asked. She looked out at the window, toward the north. "It's too far for us to fly."

Cocoa remembered the last time the fairies had seen Nillie. They had journeyed there by boat...and that was a lot of work!

"Butterscotch will fly you out

to Rock Candy Isle in the Vanilla Sea. Nillie will meet you and then take you up to the North Sea." Princess Lolli hugged the fairies.

"Supersweet," Dash said.

"Meet back here in the castle in one hour," Princess Lolli said. "You don't need to bring a thing. Nillie has taken care of everything."

Cocoa smiled to herself. She knew that Princess Lolli was talking to Berry. Berry was definitely *not* a light packer!

"And one more thing," Princess Lolli added. "This is top-sugar-secret. Not many fairies know about who Nillie really is, and we'd like to keep it that way."

"Especially when there is a troll hunting for treasures in the North Sea!" Cocoa exclaimed.

"Sure as sugar, the Candy Fairies will stick

together and not say a word!" Dash cried.

Princess Lolli smiled. "I know you will," she said. "Also, we don't want Gargo knowing that we're onto his scheming and stealing."

"Better to catch a troll by surprise," Cocoa said, thinking out loud.

"Exactly," Princess Lolli said. She winked at Cocoa.

Cocoa felt very proud—and more determined than ever to help Nillie. Gargo was likely as selfish and messy as Mogu. And she hoped he was just as easy to trick!

The fairies flew out of the throne room. Before she left, Cocoa peeked over her shoulder. She noticed a very worried look in Princess Lolli's eyes. Going to the North Sea was exciting, but Cocoa was certain there were dangers in those waters. She waved to Princess Lolli and forced herself to smile.

"We'll be fine," she called.

"I know you will be," Princess Lolli said. "But I can still worry!"

Cocoa smiled. Nillie and Princess Lolli were counting on them, and she wasn't going to disappoint either one!

3

Rocky Start

Cocoa returned home feeling very excited and a little nervous. She watered her chocolate roses and straightened up her room. The whole time, she kept thinking about Sea Fairies and water . . . and wet wings!

"Cocoa!" Melli called. "Can we fly together to Candy Castle?"

"Sure," Cocoa said. She was so happy to see her friend in her garden. "Are you feeling as nervous as I am?"

"Hot caramel!" Melli exclaimed. "I can't stop fluttering my wings. I want to help, but I've never been swimming before. I've never gotten my wings wet!"

"I know," Cocoa said. "At least we are all going together."

"What if Gargo is saltier than Mogu?" Melli said, shuddering.

Cocoa waved that thought away. "We can handle some salty water troll," she said. "Come on, we'd better get going. We don't want to make Butterscotch wait for us."

"He'll probably have to wait for Berry!" Melli cried as she shot up in the air.

When Cocoa and Melli arrived at the Royal Gardens, Cocoa was surprised to see Berry, Dash, and Raina already there.

"I know," Berry said. "You thought I would be late again. But I know how important it is to get to Rock Candy Isle as fast as . . ."

Dash interrupted her. "I see Butterscotch!" she shouted. She pointed up to the sky.

The large royal unicorn swept down into the gardens. Her beautiful wings flapped to a stop. Princess Lolli walked out onto her terrace. Butterscotch bowed her head, and the princess stroked the white spot on her nose.

"Take care of them, Butterscotch," the princess told her.

The five Candy Fairies all flew up and onto the royal unicorn's back.

As Butterscotch was about to take off, Melli heard someone calling her name. "Melli! Where are you off to?" It was Cara, Melli's younger sister, delivering caramel to the castle. She flew up to Butterscotch.

"We are off to run an errand for Princess Lolli," Melli told her.

Cocoa knew Melli wanted to tell her sister where she was going, but she had to be true to her promise not to tell anyone about Nillie and Gargo.

"Have fun!" Cara called cheerfully as she flew toward home.

"Thank you for not saying a word," Princess Lolli said to Melli. "Once this is over, everyone will know about your bravery."

"And, I hope, how we stopped Gargo," Cocoa added.

"Yes. That, too," Princess Lolli said. "Be safe and stick together!"

The fairies waved as Butterscotch took off, heading to Rock Candy Isle.

When they were above the ground, Raina leaned closer to Cocoa and Dash. "Remember how long it took us to sail to Rock Candy Isle from Candy Kingdom?" she asked.

"This unicorn flying is the best," Dash said. "And fastest!"

In the distance Cocoa saw the small island in the Vanilla Sea. She wondered how Butterscotch would be able to land on the rocky candy beach. Then she realized he would only get low enough for them to fly off. They would have to make their way to the island themselves.

"Come on," Cocoa said to her friends. "We can fly to the ground from here." She turned and nodded to Butterscotch. "Thank you for the ride!"

The fairies followed Cocoa to the pebbled beach of Rock Candy Isle.

Dash scooped up a handful of rock candy. "Mmm, traveling always makes me hungry," she said. She nibbled on the fresh, tasty treat.

"*Everything* makes you hungry," Berry said, laughing.

Melli looked around. "What do we do now? Just wait?"

"I'm sure Nillie will be here soon," Cocoa

said. But she hoped it would be sooner rather than later.

Just then two tiny heads surfaced in the water. It was Sprinkle and Bean!

"Hey, those are Nillie's twins!" Cocoa cried. "Remember them? They helped us out last time we were on the Vanilla Sea!" Cocoa ran over to the water's edge and waved at the twin sea horses. "Who's that behind them?" She squinted to get a better look.

"I think that might be a Sea Fairy!" Raina said.

Cocoa's mouth dropped open when she saw the shiny webbed wings on the fairy on Bean's back.

"I've read about Sea Fairies, but I have never actually seen one," Raina said.

"Is she green?" Melli asked. She squinted.

"Sea Fairies are aquamarine," Raina told her. "They are the color of the sea."

"Check out her wings," Dash said.

"Don't point!" Berry scolded.

The Sea Fairy moved closer. "You must be the Candy Fairies," she said. "I am Shelly, and this is Rocky." She pointed to Sprinkle. Then she looked again. "Well, Rocky *was* there." She giggled. "She's a little shy."

"Me too," Melli said.

"We are all a little nervous to meet you," Cocoa said bravely.

Shelly flew to the beach. "It's very nice to meet you, and we're so thankful you came to help. We need to stop Gargo."

"Well, that's why we're here!" Berry said boldly.

Cocoa, Raina, and Dash couldn't take their eyes off Shelly's *sugar-tacular* wings.

"I know you are not a mermaid," Dash said, "but you sure seem like one!"

Shelly laughed sweetly. "No! See? No tail!" She flew up in the air and kicked her legs. "But I do have webbed wings." She turned around so the fairies could get a better look at her wings.

"*So mint!*" Dash exclaimed. "I bet you swim superfast."

"Sometimes," Shelly said, smiling. She turned back to the water. "Rocky, come out. The Candy Fairies are really nice!"

Cocoa watched the water and saw a small pale blue fairy pop up on the surface. "Hi! I'm Cocoa, and these are my friends, " Cocoa said. She slowly introduced everyone, hoping that Rocky wouldn't be afraid.

Rocky flew up to the beach and stood next to Shelly. She bowed her head. "Hello," she said.

"Oh, you don't need to bow to us," Cocoa said. "We're not royalty."

Rocky blushed. "But you're Candy Fairies."

"And you're a Sea Fairy!" Dash gushed. "That is supermint!"

Cocoa saw Rocky smile. She could tell Dash and Rocky were going to be fast friends.

A few moments later Nillie arrived. The enchanted sea horse was even more beautiful than Cocoa remembered. Her mane was a rainbow of colors, and her body was a beautiful cotton-candy pink.

"I am so happy to see you all again," Nillie said. Her big sea-blue eyes were surrounded by long dark eyelashes. "You remember Sprinkle and Bean, right? And I see you've met Shelly and Rocky. They will bring you up to the North Sea and help you. Once you are there, you will be able to work out a plan together to stop Gargo."

"Sure as sugar," Cocoa said.

Nillie turned to her left and nodded at a silver bucket floating up to the surface of the water. "Inside this bucket is magic sea salt from my cave," she said.

"I've never seen such delicious-looking glimmering salt," Berry said, peering inside the bucket.

"This will allow you to swim like a Sea Fairy," Nillie told them. "But this sea-salt magic is dangerous if you are not careful. You must be back at the surface before Sun Dip tomorrow. The magic will begin now and then last from Sun Dip to Sun Dip."

The Candy Fairies all nodded. "Yes, Princess Lolli told us."

Cocoa was more nervous than ever. She wasn't sure they'd be able to catch the troll before the magic ran out. And she was afraid to ask what would happen if their task was not completed by Sun Dip tomorrow.

"What happens if we don't make it back here by Sun Dip?" Dash asked.

All the fairies gasped. Dash had a way of asking the most direct questions.

"You'll be a Sea Fairy forever," Nillie said. "But I am sure that will not happen."

Cocoa looked at her friends. *I'm not sure I can do this,* she worried. This task was much more dangerous than she'd thought.

CHAPTER
4

Water Wings

Shelly and Rocky carried the bucket of magic sea salt to the beach. Cocoa and her friends followed.

"I've never read or heard of any Candy Fairy becoming a Sea Fairy forever," Raina said. "I think if we listen to Nillie, we will be okay."

Cocoa believed Raina. She knew Candy

Fairy facts and history better than anyone.

"Raina is right," Nillie said. "Be back at the surface by Sun Dip and everything will be fine." She turned to Shelly and Rocky. "Please help these fairies get their swimming wings on. And remember to watch out for Sticky."

"Sticky? Who is that?" Melli asked. Her eyes were wide and she started to bite her fingernails.

"Don't worry about Sticky," Shelly said. "He might have eight arms, but he can't see all that well."

"*Eight* arms?" Dash cried.

"Sticky is a gummy octopus," Nillie said.

"A *grumpy* octopus," Shelly added.

"We try not to bother him," Nillie said.

"And we hope he doesn't bother us," Rocky told them.

Cocoa saw that Melli didn't like that answer. A grumpy gummy octopus didn't sound like a creature anyone would want to meet!

"Let's get you all in the water," Shelly said. "Who wants to be the first?"

"I'll go first," Cocoa said. She stood in front of Shelly. Her heart was beating so fast! She felt both excited and scared. Holding her breath, Cocoa closed her eyes. She felt the tingle of the magic sea salt on her wings. "It kind of tickles," she told her friends.

"Sweet sugars!" Melli gasped.

"*So mint!*" Dash exclaimed.

"What?" Cocoa said, trying to get a glimpse of her wings. She tried to turn herself around to see.

"Your wings look crystal coated," Raina said.

"They look like a Sea Fairy's wings!" Berry cried. "I want to go next!"

As each of her friends were sprinkled with the magic sea salt, Cocoa was amazed at how quickly their wings changed. But the big test would be once they got in the water.

"Now that your wings are safe," Shelly said, "it's time to learn to swim!"

"I want to go first!" Dash said, zooming up in the air.

Rocky laughed. "Wrong way!" she said. She pointed down into the water.

Dash giggled. "Oh, right," she said.

"What about breathing?" Melli asked. She was staring at the water. "How do we breathe down there?"

"Sea Fairies breathe underwater just like

we breathe on land," Shelly said. "The sea-salt magic will let you breathe just like we do."

"Come on in," Rocky called.

Cocoa and the Candy Fairies stood on the beach, looking out at the water.

"I'm going in," Cocoa said. She moved into the water, up to her waist. She felt the cool water on her wings and turned back to see her friends. They were all right beside her!

"Let's do this together," Raina said. She reached out to the other Candy Fairies, and they all held one another's hands. "One, two, three!" she counted.

Cocoa felt the water on her body and she shivered a little. Then she opened her eyes and was amazed at all the colors and candies surrounding her. There were reefs of rainbow-flavored candy coral and schools of multicolored gummy fish swimming. Cocoa let go of Raina's and Melli's hands so she could explore a little. A gummy sea horse nodded to her, and she was amazed at the bright colors of the salted caramel coral.

"Dash!" Cocoa said. "Slow down!" Her minty friend was making tons of waves by zooming around. Cocoa was surprised. "I can talk!" she said.

Raina smiled. "I hear you loud and clear," she said.

"And I can breathe normally," Melli said. She turned to Shelly. "This is *sugar-tastic!*"

Rocky motioned for the fairies to follow her. "We have a surprise for you," she said. "All the Sea Fairies wanted to meet you."

She dove through a sugar coral reef ring and the Candy Fairies followed. Cocoa couldn't believe her eyes—there were hundreds of Sea Fairies gathered together.

"Sweet caramel!" Melli said.

"I've never seen anything so delicious," Dash said, taking in all the candy.

"This is a supersweet welcome," Raina added.

"Nothing salty about this," Berry mumbled.

Rocky waved her hands. "This is all for you!"

The Sea Fairies had prepared a feast! The candies were different from those in Sugar Valley, but Cocoa noticed chocolate candies as well as rock candy and gummy candies. Everything was so colorful, and the Candy Fairies wanted to try everything. The Sea Fairies were so generous and kind!

"*So mint!*" Dash exclaimed as she munched on a mint chocolate candy. "And did you try the saltwater taffy and this chocolate clam?" She held up a piece to Cocoa.

Cocoa took a bite of the clam. "I can see why a troll would want to take this," she said. "This is *choc-o-rific*."

Shelly clapped her hands. "We're so glad that our guests from Sugar Valley could come join us, but this isn't a celebration . . . yet." She looked around at her new friends. "We've got some plans to make."

The Candy Fairies gathered around Shelly.

"We are going to take you to Great Sugar Reef," Shelly said. "That is where we plan to catch Gargo. He is moving up the North Sea, and that reef is likely to be his next snack."

"Great Sugar Reef is where we make our saltwater taffy," Rocky explained.

"We are here to help," Cocoa said. "You are very sweet to make us feel so welcome."

"And to give us so many sweet treats," Dash added.

Shelly and Rocky led the way to Great Sugar Reef in the North Sea. Now more than ever Cocoa felt how important this trip to help the Sea Fairies was. While it was fun for the Candy Fairies to be underwater, they knew there was serious work to be done. They had to trick the troll and stop his stealing!

CHAPTER

5

The Plan

When the fairies arrived at Great Sugar
Reef, Cocoa was amazed. The sparkling reef
stretched far and wide. Shelly and Rocky
settled down near a large rock at the bottom
of the North Sea.

"Tell us about Gargo," Berry said.

Cocoa looked at her Fruit Fairy friend.

Even underwater Berry's hair was still perfect! Cocoa gathered up her long hair and twisted it into a bun like Shelly's and Rocky's. She understood now why the Sea Fairies had their hair tied up. Her long hair got tangled up and floated in her face.

"The more we know about the troll, the better to make a plan to trap him," Raina added.

"He is a large troll with an even larger appetite," Shelly said.

Dash smiled. "Just like Mogu! He eats more than I ever could!"

"And he is greedy and sloppy," Rocky added. "He doesn't really swim, either. He waddles." She got up and waddled around the rock.

Cocoa laughed. "Yup, he is just like Mogu!"

"Does he have any Chuchies?" Melli asked.

Shelly and Rocky looked at each other. "What are Chuchies?" they asked at the same time.

"They are little creatures who help Mogu and steal our candy," Cocoa explained. "We'd need to know if there were creatures helping Gargo."

Raina sighed. "If I had the Fairy Code Book, I would show you," she said. "But that was not something I could bring underwater."

Rocky and Shelly whispered back and forth. Shelly shook her head. "Well," she said, "there is no one else in the sea who takes candy like Gargo. He usually eats alone."

Cocoa picked up a small chocolate clam. "We heard he loves these," she said. She studied the chocolate shell. "Oh, the shell is so pretty!"

Shelly lowered her head. "This whole area used to be covered with chocolate clams," she said. "Now there are hardly any left. The same goes for the salted caramel coral that used to be here. And without those clams and coral, our water has been losing salt."

"Salt you need for the taffy, right?" Berry asked.

"Yes," Rocky replied. She pointed to the droopy taffy plants around the rock. "This used to be our biggest crop of saltwater taffy," she explained. "But when Gargo steals the clams, he upsets the balance of the water."

"And that is trouble for your saltwater taffy," Raina said.

Shelly nodded. "Yes," she said. She swam over to the rock and held up strands of dull-colored taffy. "This used to be a healthy taffy plant," she said. "Now look at it."

Cocoa's heart ached. She knew how hard it was for the Sea Fairies to see their candy looking so troubling.

"And what about these?" Dash asked. She swam over to a sugar coral reef that had thick licorice vines.

"That is sea licorice," Shelly replied.

Dash touched the vine. "And strong and thick! Just as I hoped," she said.

The Candy Fairies shared a knowing look.

"We can use the licorice to make a trap," Cocoa explained. "Strong and thick licorice is good for catching a troll!"

Melli pulled on the thick vine. "That should hold a troll," she said.

Rocky swam over to the vines. "But how are you going to tie him? He is huge!"

"It's tough to tie up a moving target," Berry said. "But if we get Gargo some sweet treats, he will surely stand still long enough for us to tie him up."

"I hope you're right," Shelly said. "The faster we stop him, the better. If we can stop Gargo soon, we will be able to save the taffy." She looked down at the taffy plant. "But if he keeps up his snacking habit, we won't have any more taffy to save."

"We won't let that happen," Berry said.

"Sure as sugar!" Dash exclaimed.

"That's why we're here," Cocoa added. "We're going to wrap up this Gargo problem." She started to pull the licorice vines to set the trap. "When does Gargo usually come?"

"He snacks the most in the mornings," Rocky said.

"Perfect!" Cocoa exclaimed. "We have tonight to set up the trap."

"We will be ready for him first thing in the morning," Berry said.

The Candy Fairies placed the last few chocolate clams up on the sugar coral reef. Gargo would be sure to see the clams up there.

"When he reaches for these, he will be in for a surprise," Cocoa said. She showed Shelly and Rocky how to tie the vines in order to loop Gargo's leg and string him up when he stepped toward the chocolate clams on the reef. "He will be looking up at the clams," she said, "and not down at his feet."

"Sweet," Shelly said. "I hope this works!"

"I can't wait to see Gargo's face," Rocky said.

"We only have one shot," Raina whispered to Cocoa. "Remember, we need to be at the surface by Sun Dip tomorrow."

Cocoa looked down at the salt-crystal orb around her neck. Princess Lolli was watching out for them—and counting on them to save the day. But would this plan work?

"We have to try," Cocoa said. "Come on, let's get ready to catch a troll."

6

Coral Adventure

Cocoa stood back and admired their troll trap. "Now is the hardest part," she told Shelly and Rocky. "Waiting!"

"I can't believe I am going to say this," Shelly said, "but I can't wait for Gargo to come!" She started laughing.

"He is going to be a very surprised troll," Rocky told Cocoa.

"Sure as sugar!" Dash exclaimed. "Now let's have some snacks! I've been hoping for some more sea candy treats."

"Since we have some time," Rocky said, "do you want to come with me to see how taffy is made?"

"Raina, Berry, and Melli said they wanted to see how the salted caramels were growing," Shelly said.

"And I want to taste some chocolate taffy," Cocoa said, winking at Dash.

"Me too!" Dash agreed.

"Let's be back here at Great Sugar Reef tonight so we can be ready for an early morning trap," Cocoa said.

"That sounds perfect," Berry said. "Then we have all day tomorrow to watch the trap."

"Until Sun Dip," Raina said, correcting her. "Remember, we have to be back at the surface before the sun dips."

Raina, Berry, and Melli swam off with Shelly to see how the salted caramels were growing. And Rocky showed Cocoa and Dash how taffy was made.

"This is how the taffy grows," Rocky said, pointing to the coral. "Sea Fairies take the taffy and pull and knead the candy to make it smooth and soft." She gently took off a colorful piece of taffy and stretched it before placing it back on the coral.

Dash rubbed her tummy. "Delicious!" she added.

Rocky showed Cocoa and Dash how to pull the gooey candy and wrap it around the coral.

"This is hard work," Cocoa said. "You have to have strong muscles."

"The best taffy has been stretched for a few days," Rocky told her. "The more you work the piece, the better. Sea Fairies take turns pulling the candy and leaving it out on the coral for another's turn." Rocky hung the taffy she was working with on the coral. "This reef used to be covered in taffy," she said with a sigh.

"Don't worry," Cocoa said. She placed her piece of chocolate taffy back on the coral. She wrapped her arm around her new friend. "I know this plan will work and we'll catch Gargo. This place will be filled with taffy again."

"I hope you're right," Rocky said. She spun around. "Where's Dash?"

Dash zipped by them and waved her hands. "Look at me!" she cried. "These water wings are supermint fast!"

Rocky and Cocoa laughed as Dash did flips in the water.

"I guess Dash is getting the hang of her water wings," Cocoa said.

"Come check this out," Dash called. She waved her arms. "Cocoa, you have to come see this!"

"I'll finish up this piece of taffy," Rocky said, reaching for the piece that Cocoa was working on. "You can go."

Cocoa smiled at Rocky and took off after Dash. She found her in front of a *sugar-tastic* gummy reef. The colors were bold and glimmered in the water. "Sweet sugars!" Cocoa exclaimed. "Look at the red, purple, orange, and yellow!"

"It's the only gummy coral that I've ever seen," Dash replied. "And look over here!" In a flash, she swam around the coral and disappeared.

"Wait!" Cocoa said. She swam after Dash, who was in the middle of a school of gummy fish. It looked as if Dash was swimming in a moving gummy rainbow! "Come over here!" Cocoa called.

"Holy peppermint!" Dash cried.

"And check out how the coral wraps around here," Cocoa said.

"Be careful!" Dash called.

Cocoa kept going deeper into the coral. It was a sugar maze of colors and designs she had never seen. This underwater world was amazing!

"Cocoa!" Dash shouted. "Where are you?"

Cocoa peeked her head out of a hole in the coral. "This is *sugar-tastic*!"

Dash pulled at Cocoa's arm. "I think we should get back to the sugar coral reef," she said.

"We have to show this coral to Berry, Raina, and Melli," Cocoa called to her.

All of a sudden Dash squealed. "But I don't want to show them that!" She pointed behind Cocoa.

Cocoa looked over her shoulder and saw a large green gummy octopus. "I bet that's

Sticky!" she cried. "We'd better get out of here!"

She touched the salt-crystal orb around her neck. She didn't want Princess Lolli to worry—or to see that she had found some trouble!

"Follow me!" Dash called. She dipped into a small opening in the coral.

"Dash! You are smaller than I am! I won't make it," Cocoa shouted. There was no way she was going to fit through the tiny hole

Dash had swum into. But then Cocoa looked up and saw a larger opening. Just as a green gummy tentacle waved past her leg, she swam through. She jetted through the coral maze until she came out the other side. Finally, she was out of the coral and safely away from Sticky! She turned around. "Dash?" she called.

Suddenly there was a whirling, bubbling sound. Cocoa quickly realized that she was swimming in circles. She had swum right into a whirlpool!

The water was swirling in a large circle, and the strong pull of the water was making swimming very difficult. Then Cocoa caught a flash of Dash's silver wings!

"Dash!" Cocoa shouted. "Hold on!"

The two fairies were circling around quickly.

Cocoa knew she had to grab hold of something fast! They were both struggling not to get sucked down into the dark hole in the center of the whirling water.

"I'm getting dizzy!" Dash shouted.

"Me too!" Cocoa said.

She reached for a nearby piece of sea licorice and then grabbed Dash's foot. "I think I can pull you in. Swim toward me!" she shouted.

Dash flapped her webbed wings. "The current is too strong!" she said. "I can't swim to you."

"You have to try," Cocoa said. Her grip on Dash's hand was slipping. "Faster, Dash. Flap your wings as fast as you can!"

"I can't fly! I mean, I can't swim!" Dash shouted to Cocoa. "I'm stuck!"

"Hold on!" Cocoa cried. With all her might,

she willed her wings and feet to move as she gripped her friend's hand. The whirlpool was like the strongest windstorm she had ever been in!

Then suddenly she felt a strong tug on her foot. Cocoa panicked. Was it one of the arms of the gummy octopus?

"Oh no!" she cried. She never should have gone exploring in the North Sea when they were there on a mission to catch a troll! She tugged her foot away. She had to swim away as fast as she could!

7

Sticky Trouble

It's me!" Rocky shouted. "I have you! Hang on!"

Cocoa was so happy to see Rocky holding a longer, stronger licorice vine. She grabbed on to it and threw the end to Dash. Rocky tied the other end around a large rock and was able to pull them in.

"That was close!" Cocoa said when they

were safely out of the swirling water. "I didn't think we were going to make it."

"That was a whirly whirlpool," Rocky told them. "I'm sorry I didn't warn you before about those."

"It would have been so mint if it wasn't so scary!" Dash said, panting. She looked over at Cocoa and gasped. "Cocoa! The magic crystal!" she cried.

Cocoa's hand flew to her neck. The crystal was no longer there. "No!" she cried. "It must have fallen off in the whirlpool. Oh, this is going to worry Princess Lolli!" Cocoa gave Dash a look. They should not have gone exploring!

"Rocky! Rocky!" Shelly called as she swam over to them. "Have you seen Raina, Berry, and Melli?"

"Oh, no," Cocoa said. "Have they disappeared too?"

Shelly nodded. "When we returned, your friends were worried when you didn't get back to Great Sugar Reef in an hour. I told them to wait, but they wanted to find you. Sticky is usually out in these waters, and I'm not sure where they are now."

Cocoa had a sinking feeling about a large, hungry gummy octopus and her friends. "We just came face-to-face with Sticky and had a ride in a whirlpool. We wouldn't have made it out if it weren't for you, Rocky. We have to find them—and fast!" she shouted.

Shelly and Rocky quickly swam ahead of Cocoa and Dash. Cocoa felt her heart pounding in her chest. Princess Lolli had trusted them to solve this salty case, and now everything was a mess. Losing her friends and the salt-crystal orb was not what she had planned on happening!

"They will be okay," Dash said, catching Cocoa's eye. "Raina may not have the Fairy Code Book with her, but those three are smart fairies."

"But they've never been underwater," Cocoa said. "And that Sticky is pretty slimy!" She sped up, trying to keep up with the Sea Fairies. She felt tired and out of breath. "And the light is starting to change! We don't have much time until it is dark."

Swimming sure took a lot more energy than flying!

Cocoa touched her chest where the crystal had been.

"We have to find them fast," Dash said. "It's getting dark down here now."

Cocoa flapped her webbed wings. The time had crossed her mind as well. They needed to be back to the trap early in the morning to prepare for Gargo, and they had to be back at the surface by Sun Dip or they would have to stay Sea Fairies forever.

Cocoa caught up to Shelly.

"Please don't worry," the Sea Fairy said when she saw Cocoa's face. "Sticky doesn't mean any harm. His tentacles might be long and sticky, but he wouldn't hurt anyone."

"But my friends don't know that," Cocoa said. She worried about how scared her friends might be if they saw the giant octopus.

"He just might get them gooey!" Rocky added.

"Once, it took me a month to get his goo off my wings."

Cocoa kept her eyes open for clues as to where her friends might be. She hoped they were nearby. She felt terrible that they had been worried about her and Dash. If only there was a sign that her friends were safe!

Just then Cocoa noticed something glimmering in the sugar sand. She dove down deep.

"Look!" she cried. She waved at Dash, Shelly, and Rocky. They came swimming down to the bottom of the sea. Cocoa picked up a sugar-coated hair clip. "This is Berry's! They must have come this way."

"Good catch!" Dash said.

A tiny gummy crab crawled sideways over

to Rocky and pointed one of his claws to the left. Rocky snapped her fingers. "Thanks, Clipper!" she said. "Clipper saw them. They are hiding out in the old salt well down in Chocolate Cave," she said. "It's just around the chocolate coral reef ahead. Let's go check."

Cocoa had no idea where Chocolate Cave was, but she hoped it was close. She moved her wings, arms, and legs to go as fast as she could. Soon she saw the chocolate coral reef that Rocky was talking about. It snaked along the bottom of the sea for miles. Cocoa had never seen coral made of chocolate before—or any that long! If she wasn't so nervous about her friends, she would have loved to try the chocolate and swim through all the nooks and crannies.

"Follow me," Shelly called. She waved to Dash and Cocoa. "It's a little tight getting through, but this cave is a great hiding spot."

Cocoa and Dash twisted and turned just like Shelly and Rocky. They were soon under the chocolate coral reef and surrounded by large barrels for storing salt.

"This is where we keep the emergency supply of salt," Rocky said. "But now these barrels are empty."

"We have so little salt left," Shelly added. "This is why we need to stop Gargo."

Cocoa sat down on one of the empty salt barrels. How would her friends have known to come here? This was not a spot they would have found on their own. She shook her head and wondered where her friends were now. And if they were safe from a sticky, gooey green octopus.

8

Chocolate Cave

Cocoa took a deep breath. The cave had a sweet, faint scent of chocolate. For the first time ever, the smell of chocolate was not making her feel better. Once again she felt she shouldn't have been so curious about that sugar coral reef and swum off. She should have known her friends would worry about her and Dash.

She should have thought more about the time. Cocoa dragged her feet across the sandy bottom of the sea. Now her friends were in danger. Her heart ached as she looked around the cave. Her friends were nowhere in sight.

"I thought for sure they'd be here," Rocky said.

"Maybe they are hiding," Dash said, looking around at the tunnels and archways. "Maybe they are hiding from Sticky."

Dash was right. The cave had tons of places to hide. "Raina? Berry? Melli?" Cocoa called out. "Are you in here?"

She called a few more times and then heard: "You found us!"

It was Raina. She popped up from a tunnel opening, with Berry and Melli close behind.

The three of them hurried over to give Cocoa and Dash tight squeezes. "We went looking for *you*, and you found *us*!"

Cocoa was so happy and relieved to see her friends. "Are you all right?" she asked. She pulled back to get a better look at them.

"You didn't get gooed!" Dash cried. She hugged her friends tighter. "We were so worried!"

Melli grabbed Cocoa's hand. "We were worried about *you*. That is why we went to look for you." She glanced over her shoulder. "No Sticky, right?"

"Sticky couldn't fit in this cave," Rocky said, giggling. "You are safe in here."

"Dash and I should not have left to explore," Cocoa said to her friends. "We should have stayed with Rocky. We're very sorry."

"Sure as sugar, we didn't mean to cause so much trouble," Dash added.

Berry put her hands on her hips. "What happened? Where did you go?" she asked.

"After we pulled the taffy, we saw these amazing gummy fish and then Sticky showed up. We went through a rainbow maze of coral . . . and then we found ourselves in a whirlpool."

"A whirlpool?" Raina gasped.

"Sweet strawberries!" Berry said. "How was that?"

"A little too whirly," Dash told her, "even for me! We're lucky that Rocky was there to pull us out. And when we saw Sticky coming, we swam away. I guess you got away from him too."

Rocky cleared off a space on a few rocks for the fairies to sit down. "How did you know to come to Chocolate Cave?" she asked.

"How did you find it?" Shelly added.

Berry held up the salt-crystal orb that Princess Lolli had given Cocoa.

Cocoa gasped. "The crystal!" she exclaimed.

She was so relieved to see the magic crystal again.

She realized that when her friends had been in danger, the jewel had found them. She hadn't lost it. Princess Lolli was looking out for all the Candy Fairies!

"When we saw Sticky instead of you two, Princess Lolli's crystal floated down and glowed," Raina explained. "It showed us where to hide so we wouldn't get gooed."

"Now I understand how that octopus got his name," Melli said, shuddering. "He is one sticky creature! We barely escaped his goo!"

"We were able to see that you and Dash were safe too," Berry said to Cocoa. There was a tiny image of you and Dash swimming with

Shelly and Rocky, so we knew you were okay."

Melli sat down on a rock next to Dash. "We thought for sure Cocoa, of all fairies, would find a chocolate cave! We just had to wait."

"*Choc-o-rific!*" Cocoa said. She touched the crystal on her necklace. She didn't want to cause any more trouble. "I'm so glad that we found you—and the crystal! Now Princess Lolli won't have to worry. She knows we are all together and safe."

Dash clapped her hands. "But we still need to catch a troll!" she exclaimed.

"And we can't do that in here," Cocoa said, looking around, "but we can stay here for the night and get an early start. We need to finish what we came here to do!"

Shelly looked concerned. "Are you sure

licorice will hold him? He is sure to be pretty mad when he is caught."

"Yes, I'm sure," Berry said. "I've seen many licorice vines, and none look stronger than the ones you have growing in the sea."

Cocoa saw that Shelly was still unsure. No plan to catch a troll was certain—Cocoa knew firsthand how tricky trolls could be—but still, this was a good idea. "Let's get some rest," she said.

"All this swimming does make me tired," Melli said, yawning.

The fairies settled down in Chocolate Cave for the night.

Cocoa didn't think she could fall asleep underwater, and with her head full of thoughts of catching Gargo before Sun Dip tomorrow.

But her eyes got heavy, and before she knew it, Cocoa and the rest of the fairies were fast asleep.

The morning sun reflected on the sugar rocks outside the cave, shining right in Cocoa's eyes. She sprang up. "Come on, let's go string a troll! We don't have a minute to waste, " she said, waking up her friends. She shot out of the cave, with her friends close behind her.

"Do you think Gargo will take the bait?" Melli asked Cocoa as they swam.

"I hope so," Cocoa said. "This candy world is too delicious. I have never seen so many beautiful colors of candy." She turned back to look at Shelly and Rocky. "And the Sea Fairies are so kind. I wish we were here to visit and not to catch a troll."

"I know," Melli said. "There are so many unusual places to explore. I wish we had more time."

"Remember, the sea-salt magic wears off at Sun Dip," Raina warned. "As much as I love these waters and all the stories of the sea, we have to get back to Rock Candy Isle before this sea-salt magic runs out."

Cocoa knew Raina was right, but she didn't

want to return to Candy Kingdom without helping Nillie and the Sea Fairies.

"We only have one chance to catch Gargo," Melli said.

Cocoa smiled at her friend, and together the Candy Fairies, Rocky, and Shelly headed back to the trap set for Gargo at Great Sugar Reef. The sticky business of catching a troll was about to begin!

"I can't believe I'm saying this," Shelly said, "but I can't wait for Gargo to come!"

The fairies hid behind a large piece of rock candy to watch.

"Don't worry," Cocoa said. "When Gargo comes this time, we'll be ready. He won't get away with stealing anymore. The Candy Fairies will make sure of that!"

Sneaky Snack

Cocoa took Shelly's hand. "We've checked all the vines, and those chocolate clams are in the perfect spot," she whispered. "We're ready for Gargo. Why hasn't he come?"

Shelly peeked out of a crack between two large sugar rocks. "Where is he? The sun is already in the center of the sky."

"What will we do if he doesn't show up?" Rocky asked. "We have to get you five back to the water's surface by Sun Dip."

Cocoa looked up at the surface. The water made the sky blurry, but she could see that the sun was in the afternoon position. "We have time," she said bravely.

But more time passed without sight or sound of Gargo. A couple of hours later, when the fairies had almost given up hope, Rocky fluttered her wings.

"Shhh!" Shelly scolded. "I hear something!"

Grumble, grumble, grumble.

The fairies all ducked down behind the rock candy.

It was Gargo!

With his large belly and greedy grin, he

looked similar to Mogu. He stomped along the bottom of the sea. He was smaller than Mogu, but still a very big troll! The water swirled around his feet and hands as he trudged across the sandy sugar bottom of the sea. Carelessly, he walked into coral and stepped on sea candy plants. The troll had his eye on the chocolate clams the fairies had left on the highest point of the sugar coral reef.

Cocoa held her breath as she watched Gargo reach for a chocolate clam. She silently urged the troll to take a step forward with his oversized left foot. It was inches from the licorice vine loop!

"What if he doesn't take the bait?" Melli whispered.

"Oh, sugar sticks!" Shelly said. "Come on, Gargo!"

"We have to be patient," Cocoa said quietly.

The troll stopped and turned his head. Cocoa motioned for everyone to be very still. Rocky and Shelly had told them that underwater trolls were sensitive to noise. She grabbed hold of her magic crystal.

Take a step! Cocoa thought.

Gargo inched closer and closer to the precious chocolate clams. Just when he lifted his left foot, the fairies pulled the vine, and the loop tightened around Gargo's ankle. As they yanked the vine with all their might Gargo was lifted up and dangled upside down. Shelly and Rocky rolled a large rock candy onto the rope to hold it in place.

"Whoa!" he screamed. "Put me down!"

"We got him!" Rocky cheered. She rushed to face Gargo. "Gargo, no more stealing! You've caused enough harm to these waters!"

The Candy Fairies formed a circle around Rocky. Cocoa was so happy that their plan had worked. The trap had caught Gargo!

"Arrrrrrgh!" Gargo moaned.

Rocky signaled to the caramel turtles hiding in the coral to get Nillie. "We have a troll!" she said proudly. "Gargo is not going anywhere now."

"But hurry anyway!" Melli said, eyeing the upside-down troll. "He doesn't look too happy hanging there."

Cocoa looked up at Gargo. "We did it!" she cried.

"Well, let's not celebrate until Nillie and the Sea Guards get here," Raina advised.

Cocoa knew her friend was right, but she couldn't help being excited. She knew that Princess Lolli would be so proud of them.

Berry swam up toward the surface. "Look at the sun," she said, pointing up.

All the fairies lifted their eyes up toward the sky. The sun was sliding fast to the west.

"I hope those sea turtles swim fast!" Dash said.

"We don't have much time now, do we?" Melli asked, looking worried.

"Oh, please don't leave," Shelly said. "I'm not sure we can hold these vines tight without you."

Gargo was pulling at the vines. A hungry, angry troll was hard to keep still!

"The sea turtles will get the message to Nillie," Cocoa said.

The fairies huddled together on the large rock candy, keeping the vines pulled tight. They wanted to make sure that Gargo wasn't going anywhere!

"Raina, maybe you could tell us a story?" Cocoa asked. She knew Raina had so many stories from the Fairy Code Book memorized. "It would help us all keep our minds off waiting for Sun Dip if you told a good story."

Raina nodded. "I know the perfect one," she said.

"Is it a Lupa story?" Dash asked. She loved the adventure stories about the brave Candy Fairy.

"It is!" Raina said. "And I think you'll like this one."

Raina told the story of Lupa and a treasured chocolate pearl. Cocoa had heard the legend about the precious chocolate pearl and the healing powers of the gem.

"Is there really a chocolate pearl?" Cocoa asked Shelly.

"There are chocolate pearls," Shelly replied. "They are very rare and special." She turned to Raina. "You are such a great storyteller!"

"Please tell us another," Rocky said.

Dash jumped off the rock. "Don't start another story yet!" she cried. She swam toward Gargo.

"Dash!" Cocoa cried. She wondered

why Dash was rushing off. "What are you doing?"

"Gargo is eating the vines!" she shouted. "What a sneaky snack! He is going to get away! We have to do something fast!"

Cocoa had not counted on the troll being able to eat his way out of his trap! She saw the disappointment in Shelly's and Rocky's faces.

"I think I know what we can do," Cocoa said. She remembered seeing something near the sugar coral reef that might save the day. "Rocky, come with me!" she called. "We will be right back!" she said to the others. "It will take even Gargo some time to munch his way out of that licorice loop!"

Cocoa took Rocky's hand. "Remember

when we were pulling the taffy?" she asked. "There were tiny sticky strands that stayed on the coral. We can use those to make a sticky taffy net."

"Now, that is a *choc-o-rific* idea!" Rocky exclaimed. "Gargo will get all tangled and sticky if he tries to move in that!"

"That's the idea," Cocoa said. "But we need to work fast."

Together, the five Candy Fairies braided the taffy strands that Cocoa and Rocky had collected. Very quickly the fairies made a net large enough to throw over Gargo.

"What a sweet idea," Raina said when the taffy net was finished.

"And just in time!" Raina said, looking

over at Gargo munching on the vines.

"Licking lollipops!" Berry said. "This will hold him still!"

"Come on," Cocoa said. "Gargo is not going to be able to chew his way out of this net so fast."

"I hope Nillie and the Sea Guard get here soon," Melli said, looking worried.

"Gargo is a fast eater!" Dash added.

Cocoa and Dash swam back to the sugar coral, where Gargo was getting very close to freeing his trapped foot. They threw the taffy net over him. The more Gargo struggled, the more the taffy stretched and he got tangled up.

"What a taffy-terrific idea!" Shelly said, beaming. "Cocoa saved the day!"

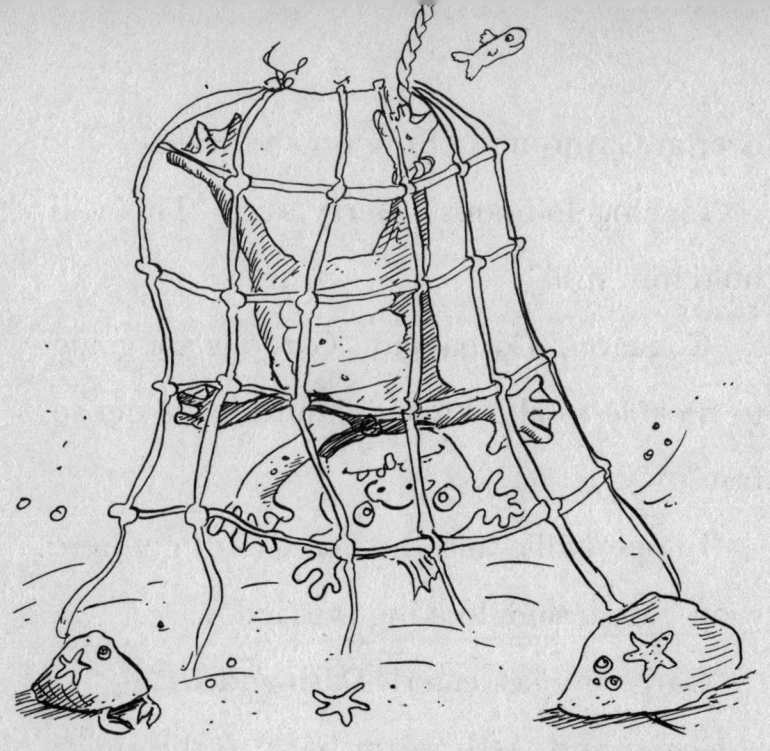

Cocoa looked around. "It was all of us," she said. She hoped Nillie and the others would arrive soon. She wasn't sure how long this taffy net would last!

10

Chocolate Treasures

A loud horn sounded. Cocoa twirled around. "What was that?" she asked. It felt as if the whole underwater world was trembling with the blaring sound. She held on to Melli's hand. She wasn't sure what was happening.

"Are you sure Gargo doesn't have any

friends who are coming to help him?" Melli asked Rocky.

"No, he is too selfish," Rocky said.

"You mean he is *shellfish*," Dash said, cracking up at her own joke.

Cocoa had to hand it to Dash for being able to joke at a time like this!

"That is the Sea Guard shell call," Shelly said. She did a double flip. "Help really is on the way!"

Cocoa squinted out into the sea. She soon saw a lineup of Sea Fairies on sea horses swimming toward them. The lead sea horse had a large conch shell around his neck, and he had stopped to blow the shell.

"I am so happy to hear that sound!" Shelly said. "The Sea Guard has arrived!"

Cocoa was relieved that the taffy net had

held Gargo tight until the guards showed up. And that there weren't more trolls on the way!

There were so many sea horses in the Sea Guard. Each fairy had her own sea horse saddle in sugar armor. They were all different

colors and very large. Each one wore a royal medal around her neck and swam in a straight line. These sea horses were smaller than the Candy Kingdom royal unicorns, but they seemed just as strong and mighty.

"Whoa, look at that sleigh," Berry said to Cocoa.

A few of the sea horses were pulling a sugar-coated sleigh with thick braided-caramel ropes. Once the cage had passed them, Cocoa spotted Nillie at the back of the lineup.

"Well done," Nillie said when she saw the fairies. "That taffy net is nice work." She motioned for the guards to move toward Gargo. The team cut the taffy net with their swords and put the troll on a large sleigh with a strong caramel net over him.

"Whaaaaaaah!" the big troll cried. "More *caaaaaaaaandy!"*

The fairies heard Gargo crying as he was carted away. They watched until the waters became still.

Shelly sighed heavily. "I hope Gargo will learn his lesson."

"Gargo will be sent to a deep-sea time-out," Nillie said. "He will have plenty of time to think about stealing and upsetting the sea salt. Perhaps he will learn a lesson or two about taking candy."

Once Gargo was gone, Shelly turned to the Candy Fairies. "Will you come visit us again?" she asked. She swam up next to Cocoa. "We all loved having you here."

"Let's plan on seeing one another again

soon," Cocoa said. "This was one of the most *sugar-tastic* adventures ever!"

"I could have done without the whirlpool ride," Dash said, circling her head. "I am still dizzy!"

"I won't miss Sticky and Gargo," Melli said, "but I will miss my new friends and my water wings!"

Cocoa smiled. She fluttered her webbed wings. Never had she imagined that she would enjoy swimming so much. She looked around the beautiful, sweet water world of the Sea Fairies. The candies and colors of the North Sea were richer than she had expected. She looked over at Rocky and Shelly. And she hadn't expected to make such good friends with the Sea Fairies. "We will come back," she said, smiling, "if you'll let us!"

"As you would say," Rocky said, grinning, "sure as sugar!"

The fairies all laughed and hugged one another tight.

"We have a gift for our Candy Fairy friends," Nillie said. She handed each of the five Candy Fairies a small box. "This is a thank-you from all the Sea Fairies here in the North Sea."

"We hope that you will wear these and think of us," Shelly added.

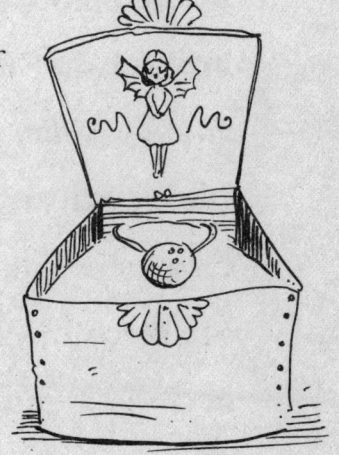

"We think you'll like them," Rocky said.

Cocoa opened up her

box. She couldn't believe her eyes. She heard Melli and Raina gasp. Berry swooned and Dash hooted. In each of their boxes was a necklace with a chocolate pearl!

"It is the most spectacular chocolate I have ever seen," Cocoa whispered. She held up the necklace and watched the delicate chocolate pearl dangle. The color and shine were so delicious! "I will treasure this forever," she told Nillie and the Sea Fairies.

"Thank you so much," Raina added. "These are truly special gifts."

Nillie swam closer to the Candy Fairies. "You have given us a great gift as well," she said. "You have saved our water and our candy."

"And you became our friends," Shelly added, grinning.

"Now we don't have to worry about Gargo," Rocky said. "And the coral and taffy will be safe in our salt water!"

"Three cheers for the Candy Fairies!" Shelly shouted.

Cocoa felt so proud. She and her friends really had made a difference in the North Sea. Sure, they had made some mistakes along the way, but they had worked together and solved the problem of a greedy, selfish troll.

"Now it's close to Sun Dip," Nillie said. "Up to the surface!"

Cocoa and the Candy Fairies all swam up and bobbed in the water. Nillie swam close and the fairies climbed on her back. "Are you ready?"

"Yes," the five Candy Fairies said.

Nillie nodded, and Rocky and Shelly sprinkled sugar dust on the Candy Fairies' webbed wings. Slowly, their true flying wings popped up and the webbed wings melted away.

"Please send my thanks to Princess Lolli," Nillie said. She touched the salt-crystal orb around Cocoa's neck. "She is a very special friend."

Cocoa couldn't help but feel a little sad. She had so loved being in the salt water with the Sea Fairies. She felt the chocolate pearl around her neck. She hugged Nillie. "Thank you," she said. "And thank you for trusting us to save the waters."

"Look, there's Butterscotch!" Dash said.

Circling above them, the caramel-colored unicorn was waiting to take the Candy Fairies back to Sugar Valley.

"You have made us all proud," Nillie said. "Now fly!"

Cocoa laughed and fluttered her wings. She leaped into the air. As much as she loved being in the water with the Sea Fairies, she was happy to be flying again. The Candy Fairies flew up to Butterscotch and climbed on her back. Cocoa smiled. She was going home with the magic salt-crystal orb safely around her neck and a treasured chocolate pearl from the now-safe salt waters of the North Sea.

Goddess Girls

READ ABOUT ALL
YOUR FAVORITE GODDESSES!

**#17 AMPHITRITE
THE BUBBLY**

**#16 MEDUSA
THE RICH**

**#15 APHRODITE
THE FAIR**

**#14 IRIS
THE COLORFUL**

**#13 ATHENA
THE PROUD**

**#12 CASSANDRA
THE LUCKY**

**#11 PERSEPHONE
THE DARING**

**#10 PHEME
THE GOSSIP**

**#1 ATHENA
THE BRAIN**

**#2 PERSEPHONE
THE PHONY**

**#3 APHRODITE
THE BEAUTY**

**#4 ARTEMIS
THE BRAVE**

**#5 ATHENA
THE WISE**

**#6 APHRODITE
THE DIVA**

**#7 ARTEMIS
THE LOYAL**

**THE GIRL GAMES:
SUPER SPECIAL**

**#8 MEDUSA
THE MEAN**

**#9 PANDORA
THE CURIOUS**

EBOOK EDITIONS ALSO AVAILABLE

From Aladdin
KIDS.SimonandSchuster.com

Making friends one Sparkly nail at a time!

All That Glitters

Purple Nails and Puppy Tails

Makeover Magic

True Colors

Bad News Nails

A Picture-Perfect Mess

Bling It On!